KB097170

Tony

in

the

Woods

Tony in the Woods

초판 1쇄 발행일 | 2019년 10월 22일

지은이 | 김학진
펴낸이 | 김동명
펴낸곳 | 도서출판 창조와 지식
디자인 | 주식회사 북모아
인쇄처 | 주식회사 북모아

출판등록번호 | 제2018-000027호
주소 | 서울특별시 강북구 덕릉로 144
전화 | 1644-1814
팩스 | 02-2275-8577

ISBN 979-11-6003-167-6   03840

지식의 가치를 창조하는 도서출판 창조와 지식
www.mybookmake.com

Tony in the Woods

HakJin Kim

Characters

- Tony Brown
- Henry Brown
- Maggie Brown
- Ben (Tony's dog)
- Ed (Tony's dog)

- Jenie (a girl in the cave)

- David Kim (Tony's friend)
- Sue Kim (David's mother)

- Becky Shaw (David's girlfriend)
- Mary Shaw (Becky's mother)

- Ali, Eli, Oli (miniature man-like figures)

1

As the sun rises over the woods, the fresh sunbeam floods into every corner of a forest cottage. In the yard of the cottage, a Border Collie rises to his feet and watches the door waiting for someone to show up. Soon, a middle aged couple appears, and the woman closes the door shouting, "Tony! Your breakfast is on the table! We're going out now."

Ben, the Border Collie, wags his tail hard greeting the couple, Maggie and Henry Brown.

"Good morning, Ben. Tony will get you breakfast. You're gonna wait, right? You're a good dog!" Henry says. They stroke his hair and go for their morning walk.

In the cottage, Tony hears his mother's loud voice and opens his eyes in surprise to see if he is late for school, but soon

sinks back on the pillow after checking the clock. "It's five, huh. It's too early to wake up. No school here. Hmm… great!" He says to himself with a smile on his lips. Minutes later, he sits on the bed and looks around his room which is much more rustic than that in town. The room is simplicity itself without any pictures, but there is a tiny window that plays a kind of painting presenting a view of distant mountains. Every morning when Tony wakes up, he needs a little time to adapt himself to the new environment.

A month ago, Tony woke up in the ordinary neighborhood and had to be at school in time as a high school freshman. He mostly was busy with his schoolwork, spending his free time outside playing basketball with his friends or doing other activities. One day he was asked by Henry and Maggie, his parents, about living in the woods together for several years. Tony was told two things; all the preparations for life in the woods were almost done and there was no problem as to Tony's education since home schooling is becoming popular as an alternative to public school education so that he had many choices for cyber- classes on the school website. Tony in his teens could understand what Henry wanted to do in his life. Henry had longed for life as a mountain man, so he had made preparation by purchasing land and building a cottage. Maggie agreed with Henry by joining him, and then they talked to Tony. Tony didn't refuse their proposal from the beginning because he loved wilderness like Henry and Maggie. When a house with three rooms and two bathrooms got finished, Tony's family moved in. Their house in town was held on a long lease and they began to stay in a cozy rustic residence.

Tony puts on boots and walks to the kitchen in which there are a glass of milk and a pancake made by wild vegetables on the wooden table. He finishes all quickly and takes dog food for Ben.

"Hey, buddy. Good morning. You were hungry and missed me all night long," Tony pats Ben on the head.

While Ben eats dog food, Tony goes to the shed to pick up a long stick before hiking. From the first day when he moved to live in the woods, he set out to explore nearby hills and mountains with Ben. Since then, he has realized how much he loves a quiet life deep in the woods, looking for things that no one knows.

After Ben empties his dog food, Tony calls Ben. "Ben, after you."

Ben runs about two yards ahead of Tony and looks back to see Tony coming. As usual, Tony walks wherever his feet take him, following Ben which always reads Tony's mind. At some point, a certain trail jumps to the eyes. Tony whistles to stop Ben at the trail that he hasn't stepped on yet. As he walks forward little by little, he feels that the trail exudes a weird atmosphere, but it looks inviting him with flowers which are blooming all around. Unlike other wild flowers that generally grow here and there, they seem to be planted and well kept by someone. Tony doesn't pay attention to the surrounding plants and passes them with no interest. He just seems to be interested in what he will see at the end of the trail expecting something. While walking with Ben, Tony looks at his cell phone and says to himself, "It's 7... I can go further for thirty minutes to not miss a morning class. By the way, this path looks odd. No one lives around here as far as I know, huh. What if we run into a wild thing like the tiger. No, it won't happen."

Ben sniffs here and there prodding next to Tony. Suddenly, Ben stops and begins to hold a thing with his paw. Tony kneels down to see what is in the dirt and lifts the thing out of Ben's paw.

"Oh, it's a necklace with a pendant of pellucid oval glass. Let me see... there's a golden letter 'J' inside the glass. This may belong to a girl. Who can drop this one in this remote place? Anyway, I'd better keep this, just in case. Who knows what this one will bring?"

Tony puts it in his pocket and thinks of Becky for a few seconds who once has been his one-way love, but becomes a friend of him after she chose David as her boy friend. While returning home, he takes pictures of the trail that he passed to make it easy for him to find the way.

As Tony comes near home, he sees that the cottage sits in the warm sunshine and nothing shatters the morning calm. On arriving at the front yard, he looks around to see if his parents are back from their morning walk.

After ordering Ben to stay outside, Tony enters his room and turns on his computer for online classes. Outside the house, Ben pricks up his ears to catch every sound while roaming around every corner of the yard and the nearby area. Ben seems to adapt to the circumstances that he has to live in his doghouse which is made by wood due to the confined space of the cottage.

A while later, Ben begins to wag his tail as soon as Maggie and Henry come into sight.

"Hey, Ben. Is Tony taking class now? You wanna play, huh? Run get this one!" Henry says and throws a Frisbee.

After smiling at Henry and Ben, Maggie goes across the

front yard and asks, "Henry, I'll get some tools for you?"

"Thanks, honey!" Henry says, throwing the Frisbee again.

Equipped with farming tools and their lunches, Henry and Maggie head for their garden in which they have spent most of the day. To grow vegetables and edible flowers was the first priority because they had to drive for an hour to buy some groceries. So they had made a sizable garden before they moved in the woods.

2

As the morning session of online classes for Tony is almost over, Ben appears from nowhere and sits on the front porch as if he knows his daily routine. Tony comes out with his lunch and Ben's snack.

"Ben, after lunch we go back to the trail. I have no class in this afternoon," Tony says and starts eating.

"Ben, are you finished? Okay! I'm done. I'm gonna text mom where I'm going. Let's go," Tony stands up from the outdoor bench.

The sun blazes down on Tony and Ben a while before they enter the woods, full of shade. Tony, dressed in a baggy shirt and jean shorts and having on a pair of black sneakers, checks his pockets and takes out his cell phone to see the photos he took in the morning.

"Ben, are we going the right direction? By the way... it isn't near our place, huh," Tony says to Ben.

Ben barks at Tony as if he understands Tony.

They have walked for an hour and reach the trail at last. The trees around it look dark green in the shade under the hot sun. While Ben is running on the trail, Tony touches a Compass app on his cell phone to figure out where he is heading. Ben, Tony's only companion in the woods, comes back to keep step with Tony.

As almost an hour passes on the trail without any new things, Tony feels bored so that he decides to go back home thinking online games.

"Hey, Ben, there's nothing interesting here. We wasted time. Let's go home," Tony says and turns around.

About a half hour after walking back Tony hears Ben barking behind, but he doesn't pay attention to it and keeps walking.

"Ben, don't stop. Hurry up! Don't take your time," Tony shouts.

A few minutes later Tony finds out that Ben doesn't come after him, and he goes back to see what's happening to Ben. He sees Ben anchor its feet in front of the tall bushes. When he goes near Ben, he can catch a glimpse of a big rock behind the bushes. A close look at it reveals a big cave that looks like a home for wild life, but the rough semi-circle entrance gives a notion that someone spent time on the cave.

"Hmm... it looks odd, huh. This definitely isn't a natural cave. Well... by the way, it's almost four o'clock. If we go in there, we'll be late for dinner. Then mom and dad will be freaked out," Tony mumbles.

"Ben, leave it for now. We'll come back some time later. Let's go home anyway," Tony says to Ben.

At the dining table in the kitchen Maggie asks, "Tony, did you go around the mountain this afternoon?"

"Yeah, twice. In the morning and in the afternoon," Tony answers.

"It means? Oh, I'm wondering if you're interested in the book about medicinal herbs," Maggie smiles.

"Yes, it's interesting. But I think it takes time to distinguish between edible herbs and inedible stuff, you know," Tony responds.

"I bet you aren't ready to teach me, huh," Tony says glancing at Maggie.

Maggie shrugs and says, "I'm studying hard, you know."

"Dad, have you looked around the woods nearby when you chose this property?" Tony asks.

"Yeah, the woods looked nice to me and mountains here aren't high and this place isn't a jungle. And the chances of you running into bears are slim. Yeah, but you can see some boars. Why are you asking? Did you find something wrong?" Henry asks.

"No, nothing's wrong. I'm just curious. Are you guys safe in the garden from boars?" Tony asks smiling at Henry.

"Sure! You saw the tall barb-wired fence, didn't you? Nothing can jump over the fence. Rather, I worry about you, Tony. Don't be reckless," Henry says looking at Tony in the eyes.

"Okay, Dad. Ben is always with me, you know," Tony shrugs.

3

Two months have passed since Brown's family moved in the woods. As days go by, Tony feels more and more excited about the routine of everyday life which looks boring to normal teens. After getting to know about medicinal herbs and how to grow vegetables, he enjoys the woods more than the time when roaming around here and there.

One Saturday morning Tony looks out the window at the gravel driveway after hearing Ben bark and finds two human figures getting out of a SUV. To his surprise, David and Becky are walking up the dusty gravel road toward the house. Tony goes outside to greet them.

"Hey, dude. How are you doing? You're a mountain teen?"

David makes a fuss.

"Yeah, the mountain's growing on me. Hi, Becky. Oh, my! What brings you here?" Tony says with a surprise.

"Tony. We haven't heard from you for a while. So we wanna see you in person how you're doing. You must be busy in this boring place, huh," David says.

"Yep. I had no time for you. Time flies," Tony giggles.

"Let's go to Henry and Maggie. It's about a hundred meters from here."

They walk past the shed to reach the garden.

"Mom, Dad, look who's here!" Tony shouts.

Maggie and Henry rise to their feet to greet David and Becky.

"What a surprise! Did your mom come here, David? Where is she?" Maggie asks.

"Hi, but mom has to leave right away this time. She promised to see you here next time," David says.

"I see. Becky, you look good. How's Mary? It's so nice to see you both. Guys, it's morning. So, take your time with Tony and Ben, and then we'll have lunch together around noon," Maggie says with a big smile.

Tony, David and Becky look at each other for a few seconds thinking what makes them have some fun in the place that has nothing but trees. At this moment Tony comes up with the trail which he has forgotten for a while.

"Hey, guys, do you wanna play games in my room or play basket ball or go hiking?" Tony asks David and Becky.

"Tony, we're in the woods. We'd rather explore nature... like searching for rare insects," Becky says.

"Yeah, let's go to the hill nearby and see what's in there," David chimes in.

"Alright, then, there's a place I've been to lately. It's just a trail, but looks odd. It takes an hour to get there. Do you wanna go?" Tony asks them.

"Sure. We can look around while hiking. But I hope we can find a shortcut," Becky says.

"Yeah, I think there must be a shortcut. Come this way," Tony says.

Tony checks the time and touches the compass, and then takes a different way from he hiked. He chooses to climb the steep mountainside to reduce the time.

About half an hour later, they catch their breath by sitting on the ground and Tony is asked whether they are near the trail. In response to their questions, Tony looks around to find the trail and finds that it lies in front of them.

"Hey, we saved more than an hour," Tony shouts.

"That sounds good, Tony. Well, where are we heading? You didn't tell us where to go," David says with a quizzical look.

"Sorry. I thought I explained where to go. We're going to the cave that Ben and I found several weeks ago. It's on this trail. It looks odd. It doesn't look natural. You'll see why I say like that," Tony says.

"We're almost there. Come on! Let's move, dude."

They stand up to keep going. While walking along the trail, Becky sees some yellow mushrooms and a lot of flowers that she has seen in a florist shop. Half way down the trail, they stop in front of bushes.

"These are bushes, Tony. Why is it special for you?" David shrugs.

"Wait, there's something behind the bushes." Tony takes David and Becky past the bushes.

"What do you see, guys?" Tony asks.

"The entrance of the cave. Well, hmm... it's big and looks

like a door which is open," Becky says with wide eyes.

"Have you seen inside, Tony?" David asks.

"Not yet," Tony says.

"Oh, I forgot a thing... my flashlight. No problem. I'll use my cell phone light."

As Tony, David and Becky step into the cave, their eyes pop at its interior. They see the smooth floor and refined walls which make them think as if they walk around in the gallery. The further they walk, the more they feel interested. Here and there light permeates from somewhere so that they can walk without cell phone flash. They keep on going forward expecting something awesome, but feeling a bit scared. At some point, David stops them and says, "Let's get out of here. I don't wanna go further. Who knows some freak things catch us?"

"Oh, that sounds possible. I'm good though," Becky says.

"Well, if you insist... it's time to go home. And I'm hungry. And you?" Tony agrees with David.

As soon as Tony suggests to get out of the cave, Ben comes right next to Tony.

4

In the garden Maggie checks her watch and shouts to Henry. "Honey, I think kids are gonna be home in no time. Come on!" At once, Henry rises to his feet and asks, "Maggie, what are for lunch?"

"Well, we have beef patties and vegetables and some sausages. Kids will love whatever I make. You know, I'm good at cooking," Maggie says.

When Tony with his friends comes near home, he sees smoke coming out of the chimney of the barbecue grill which Henry installed to prevent fire. Tony feels his mouth is watering.

"Hey, son, you're just in time. Lunch's almost ready-salads with special dressing and hamburgers and Polish sausages. How was your hiking, guys?" Henry says.

As Maggie gets outside, she smiles and says, "Tony, can you set the table? Thanks."

They all sit at the table licking their lips at the sight of the table on which tasty foods with sodas and a bottle of wine are arranged.

"Wow! Great! What a sausage! I love it. Thanks, Mrs. Brown," David says with joy.

"Yeah, it's amazing, Mrs. Brown," Becky exclaims.

"Speaking of burgers, I grilled it," Henry grins.

The afternoon in the woods passes in a pleasant mood. Everybody at the table and Ben enjoy the afternoon lunch.

As they almost finish their meals, Tony who sits facing the driveway finds a human figure that looks like a teen girl wearing a cap. He fixes his eyes on her with surprise to see where she is going. She walks fast along the driveway, but turns to the right and then crawls up the huge rock. While he thinks that she trespasses into their property for rock climbing, she disappears from sight. Tony looks around hoping to find her again with astonishment. Since it happens in a minute, Tony even doubts that he indeed saw a girl who seemed to appear on the road on foot.

"Tony, did you see a ghost, huh?" Becky asks.

"What? What makes you say so?" David asks Becky.

"I saw his jaw dropped. So I looked back to check who was coming. No one was there," Becky shrugs her shoulders.

"Well, I like your imagination, Becky. Sorry, I've nothing to say for now," Tony says with his palms up.

"If I get something amazing, I'll let you know by texting you, Becky," Tony smiles.

Tony seems to enjoy the afternoon with David and Becky, but he can't make the teen girl go away from his mind.

5

Next morning Tony gets up before hearing Maggie's shout. After having an early breakfast, he is poised to go out to search for the teen girl who climbed the rock. He doubts that he can find her in the mountain, but at least he has to do something to satisfy his curiosity. Tony texts Maggie who is still in bed that he won't be late for lunch.

Inhaling the fresh air of the forest at dawn, Tony with Ben sets off for the cave where he guessed at as a prime spot to find the girl, hoping she wasn't an illusion. Since he knows of a shortcut, it takes less than an hour. At the entrance, he takes a deep breath thinking what if he runs into a monster, but he walks in without hesitation. Everything looks the same as that of yesterday except a lighted lamp which gives out a soothing glow.

At that moment he sees a tall, good-looking girl coming toward him. She is wearing a loose yellow striped T-shirt, tight blue slacks, and a blue cap. He steps back a little and says, "Oh, I'm sorry for breaking in. I didn't mean to scare you. I came in 'cause it looked like a cave. We're going out."

"It's okay. I just didn't expect you this early. But, as long as you're here, I've got to say I've been waiting for you since you moved in with your parents. Don't be surprised. I'm just a teenager like you. By the way, I am Jenie."

"Oh, you already knew me! I'm Tony Brown and this is Ben."

"Ben. You're cute," Jenie pats the dog on the head.

"Well, it may sound odd, but I've needed a friend in the woods and I happened to see you. So I dropped my necklace to catch your attention, but it didn't work. At last, yesterday I showed up in the driveway on purpose to draw your attention," Jenie says with a smile.

Tony loses his tongue when he hears Jenie, feeling a bit

afraid. He wants to get out of there, let alone his curiosity about her. Being unaware of his feeling, she continues to say, "Do you wanna see how I live here?"

Tony nods and follows her with Ben.

They walk to the end of the cave and Tony sees a wooden bed at the corner which is surrounded by a tall fence and draped with fine mesh cloth. He wonders how the bed could be built inside the cave.

"Jenie, don't tell me you worked on this wooden bed," Tony says with a look filled with doubt.

"Yeah, I did. Come this way. The cave has two entrances--the one you passed through and this back door. Building materials were brought through the back door that keeps from animals, and it gives on to the other side of this mountain. Maybe I can tell all the details later on," Jenie says.

"Wow! You're amazing. Jenie, I think you're my age. Then, how does your education go?" Tony asks.

"You know, I'm a high school senior. I'm living with a foster family. It's been almost three years to be with them. The nice lady, a single parent, allowed me to live until I go to college. You know what? I got a full scholarship to college. I don't remember about my birth parents 'cause I was raised in a foster care," Jenie answers without any emotion.

Tony wants to ask her which high school she goes to, but he skips it and says, "I see. Let me ask you this. How could you climb the rock so quickly?"

Jenie smiles and says, "I've rock climbed since my childhood. Well, Tony, I wanna be a friend if you let me."

"Oh, cool. I'll hang out with you when you come here," Tony says.

Jenie seems delighted a lot. Soon, Tony asks whether Jenie can join him for lunch with his parents.

"Tony, thanks, but next time. Your parents will be frightened 'cause they can't imagine my situation," Jenie refuses his offer politely.

After a little pause, Tony excuses himself by saying he has a lot of reading assignments to finish for his term paper.

On the way home Tony feels a little uncomfortable with Jenie since he has never expected to have a friend in the woods.

Besides, she seems to be different from other girls like Becky. Speaking of his curiosity, it comes to be a kind of bother.

When he arrives at the cottage, he heads to the garden to check his parents are working. He sees them planting some flowers and trees. Tony rolls up his sleeves to help them without saying a thing. He has no intention of talking about Jenie. Rather, he makes up his mind to keep things about her in secret.

6

Jenie stands still watching Tony and Ben until they disappear from view, and then she enters the cave. After she locks the gate of the fence, she goes out through the back door and climbs down with agile legs to the lot where she parked her scooter, her valuable transport to reduce the time it takes to commute from the town to the cave.

Jenie arrives at a small town where she has settled down since she was placed and raised in foster care. It sits about five miles from Tony's hometown. In the town she heads straight to an indoor rock climbing gym to do part time job as an assistant though it starts about 3 o'clock. Every Sunday she works with the equipment and sometimes helps climbers in class. She feels proud of herself on her sports ability which has been formed through her own efforts. Doing errands in many foster homes without any complaints made her body strong and agile. Thank to her circumstances, she grew up as an all-around athlete. Now she is doing a good job in the team winning on the track in high school, and surprisingly, she earned a full scholarship to college due to her straight As.

Sitting on the bench of the locker room while waiting for the class, Jenie thinks back to her childhood for the first time in years. Jenie remembers how she has been well behaved so far; she has never made any trouble and thanked each foster family for providing food and bed. But, she sometimes felt blue when she came to think of her sad life that she hadn't got the summer break most kids got. She worked part time almost every day after school to make extra money. And every time she felt lousy she overcame by running and climbing on everything in front of her. As she grew up, she saved up little by little and could afford to buy a scooter. With her scooter, she ran around neighboring areas and found the mountain which seemed to be good for rock climbing. And while roaming around mountains, Jenie found a big cave covered with grass and small trees. Oddly enough, she thought it was her home. At first she thought it was a cave with rock formations, but it seemed like someone dug into the side of a low hill to make a dwelling place because of its lofty entrance and its spacious interior. After she checked that there was no trace of living things including human beings, she didn't care what would happen next and began to make a wooden bed and a fence with dried up trees left around the cave.

When she almost finished the bed and a fence, she happened to see Tony's family move in the woods and began to feel close to them. While stealthily observing the family, she began to have a feeling that the friendship with Tony will be worth to her. Since then she watched and followed Tony and gathered some information about Tony whenever she stayed in the cave. She had no idea how to get along with him, but she just tried what she could do like she had survived the world as an orphan.

Now Jenie feels a sense of community that she had never experienced because she started her life in a foster home as an abandoned baby who was found at a social welfare facility.

Though she knows that there are only three months left to spend with Tony in the woods, she considers Tony as one of her best friends as well as a younger brother who she can see any time in the future.

As the rock climbing class begins, Jenie busies herself with people in class. She helps trainees to grip rocks and guides how to step on a small rock to climb the wall. She focuses on what she is supposed to do, forgetting about all that happened in the morning.

Meanwhile, Tony spends his time with Henry and Maggie doing things in the garden. He focuses on working as if he forgets meeting Jenie at the cave in the early morning. Living in the woods is meant to be working without an idle thought. Three of them work all day long except during meals, and at sundown they sit at the kitchen table.

"Tony, you were a big help today. You're quick and powerful. Now, you're a man, huh," Henry says.

"Yeah, we couldn't do things that much without you, Tony," Maggie agrees quickly.

"I enjoyed it a lot, Mom. Oh, it's time to watch a baseball game, Dad. It's already started," Tony says turning to his cell phone.

They begin to get involved in their cell phones. They talk occasionally with their eyes fixed on their phones. The night grows dark, and Maggie says to two men, "You should get some sleep."

As the dawn breaks, Tony turns off his alarm clock as soon as it goes off and falls asleep again snoring since he worked like a dog on the previous day. About an hour later, he just sits on the chair to have breakfast but dozes off hearing Maggie who says that she is going to the town with Henry.

"Hey, listen. Tony, do you wanna go? You can take Ben," Maggie says.

"To the grocery store?" Tony asks with his eyes closed.

"Yeah. And we'll pick up a dog for Ben. We think he needs a friend for night in here. He must be scared when staying outside alone," Maggie says.

"Good for Ben. Yep, I'll go with you though I have to skip my morning class. But I can catch up with it this afternoon. Today's Monday. So... I have time," Tony says.

Henry drives his van to the town. They stop by at a grocery

store first and then go to the house where Maggie already called for the appointment to adopt a young trained Border Collie, the same species as Ben. After picking up the new one, they put him with Ben in a pet cafe to have lunch before going back home. In a restaurant they talk about naming the new dog. Tony suggests that he'd like to call the new one Ed. Henry and Maggie agree with Tony about that.

On the way home they pass a small town and Tony looks out the car window at small scaled buildings along the street.

"Jenie may live in this town," Tony says without thinking.

Maggie asks Tony immediately. "Who's Jenie? I haven't heard of her. She must be going to the same school as you 'cause kids in this town go to your school."

"Really? I didn't know that. But... it doesn't matter now. Actually, I don't know her exactly, so I've nothing to say," Tony shrugs.

"Yeah, okay. Anyway, this town is very small, so we can't help driving to our town to shop," Maggie says turning her face to Tony.

On arriving at the cottage, Henry begins to gather some leftover planks in the shed. He starts to make a doghouse for Ed and rework Ben's doghouse by putting a plastic waterproof cover over the roof and on the floor. Tony gives up taking online classes to help Henry. It takes up a whole afternoon to finish two doghouses. When they are done and placed side by side, Ben and Ed seem to show their gratitude by wagging their tails and licking Tony's hands.

"Hey, guys. I made this. Tony just helped me, huh. From now on, spend all your time together. You both don't have to worry about raining. Are you happy?" Henry rubs Ben's and Ed's heads.

That night it rains hard as if it has waited until the roofs of doghouses are waterproofed. Ben and Ed stay together in Ed's doghouse with the mesh door shut. The door was Tony's idea to keep his dogs in safe at night, and funnily enough, Ben knows how to use it.

As the rain gets heavier, Tony can't fall asleep and looks outside the window setting his elbows on the windowsill. He sees the rain lash the earth in the soft light coming from lamps which Henry installed on two columns. While he stares at a rain streak, it suddenly reminds him of a yellow striped T-shirt. Jenie in that shirt looked strange to Tony because most girls don't wear that kind of shirts. Tony feels pity on Jenie who has survived the world being abandoned without parents' love. As he keeps thinking of Jenie, he finds himself waiting for the coming weekend to see her.

8

The next day, Tony sets off to look into the cave to get more information about Jenie. Now that she comes into his life, he can't ignore what he heard from her. He has to see how she can stay in the cave every weekend.

On climbing the mountain, Ben and Ed lope along in front of Tony, and Ben doesn't look back at Tony this time. He seems excited with Ed, his companion that Ben has had for the first time. They stop at bushes outside the cave and run around nearby sniffing disinterested in Tony. After watching them for a moment, Tony turns to the cave to get in. There, he finds a small door which is half open. He tilts his head a little wondering who installed this door because he has never noticed it during his visits. He gets a little nervous thinking what if living things live in this place, unnoticed by Jenie.

Tony walks slowly into the cave and looks in every nook and corner. Nothing looks special except lights coming in through slits which don't seem to be natural. As he goes deeper, he feels flickering shadows around him. He tries to find out who is behind after checking Ben and Ed are not around him. A little while later Tony catches sight of tiny toes under a thin rock. Those toes tell something that will astonish Tony. Tony halts at the spot wondering which creature has that tiny toe. When he sees it close at hand, he finds there are three pairs of five toes. Instantly he steps back in fear of things, envisioning himself who is surrounded by tiny blood sucking monsters. As he moves backward about three yards, three things finally reveal themselves and come toward him. Each one is a foot tall with bare feet. They look like hairy men but they are too small. Tony stands staring at them thinking what to do with them. He looks back for a second to see if he can make it to the entrance. At that point Ben and Ed show up and run toward Tony, and those miniature man - like figures are gone in a flash.

"Hey, guys. Where were you? You missed them. Does Jenie know them? We'll see," Tony says to dogs.

Tony continues to walk to the gate of the fence and grabs the knob. While he is hesitant to open it, the gate opens itself. This time he isn't shocked, rather, he thinks that it's a chance for him to communicate with those hairy creatures. As expected, Tony sees three miniature man-like figures sit close together on the bed and look up at Tony. At that moment Ben and Ed begin to growl at them. Tony blocks dogs and have them get out of the fence. As soon as Tony turns to the figures, the one near the door sings, "Sit down, Tony. I'm Ali and they are Eli and Oli. We know you and your family."

With astonishment Tony says, "What a surprise! You speak English. Your voice sounds like music. Anyway who are you? Are you small people or what? Are there more guys like you in the mountain?"

"Yes, we live in a community. We live on insects and vegetables. We don't know what we are. We just look like you, but we don't cook nor live in the building. We are half monkey and half mole, but superior to both and more similar to the man," Eli sings in English.

"I see. I wonder how you can speak language. Where did you learn it?" Tony asks.

"We don't know. We just speak when we begin to crawl around the trees," Oli answers.

"Oh, I get it. Anyway, it's amazing to hear you sing in English," Tony says with eyes open.

"By the way, why are you here? Are you living here with Jenie?" Tony asks again.

"No, she doesn't know about us. She doesn't know we helped her make this bed and a fence," Oli sings.

After hearing them, Tony doesn't understand how these miniature man-like figures helped Jenie, but he passes it. Now it's time for Tony to ask what brings them to the cave this afternoon. He is told that Jenie has been the only person that they have cared for since they found her struggling to survive the hard situation she'd been in. And now they want to do something meaningful for her because she will be away from the woods in less than three months. And then they ask if Tony has any intention to make her feel happy, adding that they will support Tony no matter what he does.

After a while, Tony calls Ben and Ed to go home. On his way home he can't believe what happens in the cave doubting that he dreams in broad daylight.

9

At night Tony can't sleep thinking of three hairy miniature man-like figures--Ali, Eli and Oli. He feels he becomes an 'Alice in Wonderland.' He wonders how such odd human shapes exist on earth, unknown to the world. In addition to their shapes, the sound of their voices was overwhelming because it was like a musical performance when they talked in turn. Feeling like Tony hears their voices all over the room, he turns his thoughts to Jenie. Considering what he was asked to do for Jenie by them, he starts feeling uncomfortable about one thing or another and wonders if he can cope with this situation. The more he thinks about them, the less he understands.

Saturday has come at last for Tony to be able to see Jenie.

Though Tony hasn't been disposed for being Jenie's friend, he needs to talk to her about what he experienced this past Tuesday. He remembers that Ali with his friends didn't ask Tony not to disclose their existence to Jenie. From the morning Tony busies himself doing chores and playing with two dogs. He thinks that he should have asked Jenie's cell phone number. For now he has no idea how to meet her unless he waits near the cave. Then he sees two people coming in the distance. He wonders if Jenie's coming with her friend. To his surprise, David and Becky again show up at Tony's home in a week.

"Surprise! Here are sandwiches and a cake for you!" Becky says and raises her both hands with plastic bags.

"Oh, that's great! Thank you so much. Let's get inside. Mom and dad went to the woods, but they'll be for lunch," Tony says.

Tony brings them some homemade drinks when they are seated in the kitchen.

"Hmm, what's this? It's sweet. By the way, how are things going in the cave?" David asks.

"Oh, the cave... I went there with Ben and Ed and found

things," Tony says hesitating for a moment.

"What? Things?" Becky asks with surprise.

"Before I tell you, I have to ask you something, Becky. By any chance, do you know Jenie, a senior in your school?" Tony asks.

"You mean a tall girl who is good at indoor rock climbing? I've never talked to her 'cause I have no chance to bump into her. But girls who are on the swim team said she's the best person in that area. Why are you asking?" Becky asks.

"Well, that's a long story. Since last Sunday I've been totally lost. Still I can't believe what I saw. Anyway if I tell you the story, you have to keep it in secret. Can you do that?" Tony says.

David and Becky nod their heads with eyes full of curiosity. Tony talks about Jenie first and then hairy miniature man-like figures. David and Becky listen to Tony without missing a single word. When Tony finishes the story, David asks, "Do those miniature figures stay in the cave all the time?"

"I guess not. They said they live in a community, but didn't say where. Can you do me a favor? Becky, let me have Jenie's cell phone number," Tony says to Becky.

"Sure, I'll ask a friend of mine if I can have it. By the way, are you gonna do what you were asked by dwarves?" Becky asks.

"I think so. Becky, they have names--Ali, Eli and Oli. Well, I think I have to do something for her 'cause I'm a little afraid of them. They seem to have pity on Jenie who was abandoned and had to stand on her feet. And I was also moved by her story."

"Now I feel much better after sharing with you. For the past several days, I couldn't concentrate on anything. So, I was gonna text you. Well, do you have any idea to make Jenie happy before she leaves for the college?" Tony says.

"Let's put our heads together, guys. I think she needs money when she goes to college. How about holding a charity event for Jenie?" David says.

"By doing what?" Becky asks.

"Yeah, that sounds good to me. Is there a rock climbing wall somewhere in town?" Tony asks.

"Yeah, I remember a small park where my family went for

an outing. I saw a rock climbing wall though I just enjoyed a swimming pool and a giant water chute. What's in your mind?" David says.

"Is it in town? If yes, let me see... first of all we have to ask the state and natural resource agency for holding an event. David, get there and talk to a personnel whether it's possible. I'm gonna ask Jenie to perform rock climbing," Tony says.

"Okay, I'll go with David. Tony, can we go to the cave after lunch?" Becky says, smiling.

10

Having sandwiches and cake in the woods is a bit amusing. Henry and Maggie also enjoy them so much, and they've polished off the whole cake.

"Becky, say thank you to Mary for lunch. We appreciate it. She should have been here with us. Soon, I'll hold a small party when mulberry wine's ready to drink," Maggie says, smiling.

"Mom, Dad, we're gonna walk around the house. See you in the evening," Tony says.

This time two dogs stand behind Tony as if they don't have to protect Tony because of David and Becky.

Tony, David and Becky set off the trail to reach the cave crossing the ground baked hard by the sun. As soon as they enter the forest, they feel a refreshing breeze coming from the mountains.

As three of them almost get to the cave, they see some things moving around trees. The things are in and out of sight, and they keep a certain distance from them. To their surprise, they turn out to be miniature man-like figures. Becky whispers, "David, they must be dwarves, but they are so tiny that they look like elves. Are they real? Are they welcoming us? Do you think so?"

"Yeah, I think so. They really look bizarre enough to frighten Tony in the first place," David whispers to Becky too.

And David turns his head to Tony speaking with his eyes. Tony nods his head to him and turns to miniature man-like figures, "Hello, it's nice to see you again. These are my best friends, Becky and David. We share everything, and you know we keep secrets as long as I live in the woods." Instantly, they respond together, "We knew you would bring your friends. Welcome to the woods." At this moment David and Becky understand how Tony feels about them.

All of them sit on the rock instead of getting in the cave.

Ali opens his tiny mouth and sings with his amazing voice, "It's the first time to talk to people after Tony. We knew Jenie, but we never showed up in front of her yet. It's nice to see you. My name is Ali and they are Eli and Oli."

"Hi, nice to meet you, Ali, Eli and Oli," Becky says and extends her right hand.

Ali smiles, but refuses to accept it.

"Well, Ali, I and my friends discussed how we can make Jenie happy. And we decided to hold a charity event at a small park. Considering her as an active sportswoman, we think she'll be satisfied if she's involved in an area such as rock climbing for bystanders while we sell our valuable merchandise and some goodies with beverages to raise money," Tony says.

"That sounds good. Did Jenie say okay? If she does, we're okay with it," Eli sings.

Sitting in a daze, David and Becky look at Tony with eyes of meaning saying in silence "Are we with aliens now?" At once Tony shrugs his shoulders, and says, "Thank you for your support. We'll do our best. By the way how can I get in touch with you to inform you about the date of the event."

"Oh, we'll do in our own way. We'll be always with you. So you can do whatever you want," Oli sings, smiling.

"Okay, then we'll start as soon as I talk to Jenie and move ahead with what we discussed," Tony says.

"David, Becky, do you have anything to say to these guys?" Tony asks, pointing to miniature man-like figures with his palms upward.

"Well, do you mind if I ask a personal question? Where are you from?" Becky asks in a small voice.

"We live in another world you can't belong to," Ali sings.

"Oh, I see. Thanks," Becky says in confusion and rises to her feet.

Soon after, David stands up following her without saying a word. He has been quiet while hearing the whole conversations. David's just observed Ali and his friends with awe thinking that miniature man-like figures are an alien species from another planet.

"It was nice meeting you all. Thank you," David says at last and leaves the trail with Becky and Tony.

All three teens are at a loss for words since they get out of the trail.

"You see! I told you so. They look like monkeys without tails, but they sing in English. There isn't such a talking creature on Earth, huh, so I called them miniature man-like figures," Tony opens his mouth.

"Yeah, we believe you," David and Becky say at the same time.

"Oh, we should have checked the cave to see if Jenie's come. I was so shocked by their sudden appearance. So, I forgot that," Tony exclaims.

"Calm down, Tony. I'll try to get Jenie's number right now," Becky says and texts to her friend.

Soon, Becky who has a good relationship with lots of friends receives Jenie's cell phone number.

"I sent it to your phone, Tony," Becky says.

"You're a big help, Becky. Thanks a lot," Tony says.

11

As Tony sees off David and Becky, Tony texts, "Hi, this is Tony. I happen to get your number. When you get to your place, text me." Soon he receives an answer from Jenie, "I'm on my way. I'll see you on the driveway of your house. It takes twenty minutes."

Tony sets the alarm five minutes ahead of time. While waiting for Jenie, he checks where Henry and Maggie are and calls Ben and Ed. At once they come up to Tony wagging their tails and then run across the lawn together to catch the Frisbee Tony flicks to the side of the front yard. A while later Ben and Ed begin to take turns catching it though Tony doesn't order to do it. Tony smiles at them and says, "Good dogs! How smart you are!"

The time comes and the alarm goes off. After Tony silences it, he walks down the driveway. Ben and Ed follow him placing the Frisbee on the lawn. As he reaches the end of the driveway, he sees Jenie coming on her black scooter. He thinks she looks awesome with her black boots.

"Hey, you texted me, huh. How did you get my phone number?" Jenie says, smiling.

"Becky, my friend, got your number. You look awesome." Tony says.

"Hey, Ben! Oh, there's another Border Collie," Jenie says, patting Ed on the head.

"It's Ed. Do you wanna see my parents now?" Tony asks.

"Well, not this time. Sorry about that," Jenie says.

"That's okay. Today, I have something to talk about. Jenie, I don't know you well, but I wanna do you a favor before you go to college. How about that?" Tony says checking her mood.

"It's very kind of you, thanks. By the way, what are you planning for me? I'm curious about that," Jenie says plainly, but she seems to feel embarrassed.

"Before discussing, we'd better go to the trail unless you

come to my place," Tony suggests and says to two dogs, "Go home!"

Jenie drives her scooter carrying Tony in the rear. After she parks it in its regular place, they walk up the hillside. From the parking place it takes only fifteen minutes to get to the back door of the cave. The trail which Tony walked from his house extends past the other side of the cave to somewhere unknown.

Jenie unlocks the back door and leaves it open after she takes out a stool from inside.

"The room is too small for two. Have a sit, Tony. It's nice to breathe here, isn't it? I love this forest. It's thick, but not too dense. Most of all, I met you," she says looking Tony in the eyes.

"Yeah, there's more than you imagine. Right now I see them," Tony says looking up the sky to see if there are miniature men.

"What do you mean? You mean big animals like bears or other weird things?" Jenie says with big round eyes.

For a moment Tony hesitates to tell her about Ali and his friends, but feels that they don't have a problem with it and they must be nearby. So, Tony tells Jenie all about what happened in the cave.

Jenie looks calm after knowing the existence of miniature men. She seems to understand how she could build the wooden bed on her own.

"Tony, it's surprise to hear their existence from you. You know, I survived in the world without parents. So, I'm not afraid of anything. Well, I wanna see them. Are there around here?" Jenie asks.

"I think you'll see them soon 'cause they must be here," Tony says looking around trees.

A few minutes later Eli shows up and the others come down from a tree and stand on the large flat rock across Jenie. Jenie steps back a little with surprise as she sees his humanlike but weird figure, but she looks a bit excited by his voice when Eli starts to sing.

"Oh, you're singing when speaking. It sounds so good. First of all, I thank you all. How generous you are! I really feel gratitude for caring for me," Jenie says.

"Don't mention it. We love you, Jenie." They sing together.

Jenie smiles at them and then listens to Tony about the charity event that Tony and David planned. He says that every plan can be changeable according to Jenie's thoughts.

She looks at Tony and says, "The plan is great. I'm gonna do rock climbing three times and let people do rock climbing during my breaks. Of course, I'll help each of them."

"And I'm gonna ask my boss if I can borrow equipment for rock climbing," she adds.

"Then we'll make rules, like those who buy stuff over ten dollars can do it. What do you think?" Tony says.

When Tony and Jenie make conversations, Oli meddles in awkwardly, "We'll be there. We won't show up in front of people. We'll just watch and enjoy it on the tree. Do you mind?"

"No! You're welcome anytime. By the way, can I ask where you're from? I'm just wondering 'cause I've never met your people," Jenie says calling them people.

"We're from somewhere you never imagine. It's what I can say to you," Eli sings.

Jenie nods her head and smiles back at them.

12

As the summer break has begun, preparations for the charity event are underway. David does his job as a coordinator with Becky, and Tony who is housebound unless his parents give him a ride just texts them to know how things work. So far Tony has never mentioned to his parents about Jenie nor miniature man-like figures, thinking they'd rather be blind.

Everything for the event is set on one summer day. Due to various circumstances the event is held in late July, under the summer heat.

Tony arrives at the park first thing in the morning with his parents who promised to support Jenie while hearing about her several days before the event. Feeling the warm breeze, Tony looks up the cloudless blue sky and says, "Um... I feel the warm air from the morning. Mom, Dad, are you gonna stay here all day? Or come back to pick me up?"

"I can sleepover at David's house tonight if you allow me," Tony says to Maggie.

"Okay, no problem. But we'll stay as long as we want. Remember, be always careful! Oh, here comes David and Sue" Maggie says.

As Sue stops her van at the parking lot, Henry opens the backdoor to take out things.

"Hi, Sue, how are you doing? Long time no see! We're sorry we couldn't share heavy stuff," Maggie says when Sue gets off the van.

"Oh, don't mention it. It's nothing, and you donated enough money, huh," Sue says waving her hands and smiles.

"You know what? I made lunch for all of us, homemade pancakes and special salads," Maggie giggles.

While two women talk, three men are busy taking out outdoor tables, their favorite collections to sell and snacks. Soon Mary and Becky join them with beverages.

All of them carry the stuff for the event to a designated area where rock climbing wall is nearby. They arrange outdoor tables setting drinks and snacks and a lot of stuff they have cherished. Three teens spent their savings willingly for Jenie and their parents have been pleased to help their kids by money with warm support. Everything in the park looks good for Jenie.

At last Jenie shows up on her black scooter and joins them.

"Hi, Tony, Becky and David, you're early. Oh, let me introduce myself to you, Mr. and Mrs. Brown...," Jenie says, smiling.

"Oh, you're Jenie. It's nice to meet you. I'm Maggie and this is Henry. Sue and Mary," Maggie says, smiling.

Sue and Mary greet Jenie waving hands.

"You're the star today. We've been expecting your performance. Oh, don't feel pressure," Mary says making a fuss.

Jenie smiles at three mothers and says, "Thank you so much for this awesome outing. I was excited a lot when I was offered this event, and I'm deeply moved by your supports. I won't forget your caring about me." Soon, Jenie goes to the rock wall and places mattresses on the ground which have been equipped for rock climbing in the park. After she looks around taking a deep breath, she begins to exercise and do some warm up stretches.

Around ten o'clock a bunch of young people gather around the rock wall and they order some snacks and beverages at the outdoor tables. While Tony and David are busy at each table, Becky stays near Jenie to do an errand.

As Jenie climbs the wall by stepping small colored stones riveted on it one by one, young bystanders seem to be fascinated and they begin to buy things for over ten dollars to get a ticket for a try. So, most of the stuff they prepared is sold in the early afternoon and snacks are almost running out. Henry and Maggie leave for the store to replenish more supplies for tables. Most park goers stop by at the rock climbing wall to watch Jenie's performance. During the intermission, Jenie becomes busier with participants who want to try to climb the wall. Jenie hasn't had a break time from the morning until her last performance, scheduled as the finale of the event. When the time comes for Jenie to do the third performance, she looks tired a bit. But, on the rock wall Jenie is so good at climbing the wall like a spider. She receives a loud cheer from spectators when she touches the ground. She smiles on spectators and turns around after people scatter over the park.

She takes a few steps toward Tony, smiling on her lips. At that moment Becky says to David, "Hey, did you see Ali or Oli? I haven't seen them anywhere around us."

"We were so busy that we couldn't think of them. I think they've been watching us throughout the event," David says.

In an instant, David sees Jenie stumble a little before Tony and falls to her knees. While Tony opens his eyes wide in shock, Ali, Eli and Oli show up out of nowhere.

"Tony, look at us. Don't be panic. She's not dead. She just passes out. Don't let them see us. Put your shirt on us," Ali sings in a low voice.

As Tony puts his shirt on miniature men located on Jenie's chest, Mary and Sue come running to see what's happening.

"Oh my gosh, she fainted. Is she breathing? Call 911. It's really hot," Mary says, at a loss.

"Mom, don't fuss, please. She's just exhausted, and she'll be fine," Becky says.

13

Tony and David lay Jenie on one of the outdoor tables as Ali gives an instruction. And they stand next to Jenie watching Tony's shirt which covers Jenie's chest. They wonder what miniature man-like figures are doing under the shirt. A quarter of an hour later they see Jenie lie with half closed eyes.

"Jenie, are you okay?" Tony says touching her shoulder.

"What happened? Why am I lying on the table? Oh, I was out of consciousness, wasn't I? It was so hot," Jenie says, sitting up.

At the same time Ali, Eli and Oli crawl out of the shirt and sing, "Hi, guys, we're here."

"Oh, you were here with me. I heard songs for a while in my sleep. Thanks to you all, I feel so happy. Oh, thank you so much for everything," Jenie says with tears of joy in her eyes.

After the event is over, Mary drives home alone with her stuff while Sue takes David with two teens to her house. Jenie is also invited to David's home for a sleepover. On the scooter ride Jenie thinks of Tony feeling a sense of belonging. She says to herself, "I'm a really lucky girl."

In the late afternoon, Tony, David, Becky and Jenie go to the mall on foot to congratulate themselves on finishing the event successfully. Becky buys hamburgers and soft drinks. While eating they are excited to spend time together all day, they seem to be proud of their roles done in the park. As four of them feel closer to each other than before, they express their own emotions and thinking. As David and Becky hear Jenie's whole life from her mouth, they feel sorry for her, having to adjust to a harsh environment.

Late at night four of them arrive at David's house for a sleepover. Since they are on their summer break, they feel easy about sitting up all night. In a big guest room Jenie and Becky sit on the couch side by side. When Tony and David get in the room to set the table for pizza, Tony says, "Wow! You girls look alike. You look like sisters, huh."

"Really? I didn't realize it. Now that you mention it, I see Jenie and I are blue eyed and blond," Becky says.

"Yeah, Tony's right. Now I can see that," David says.

Jenie smiles at them looking up two boys and shrugs her shoulders.

"Come on! Let's do something fun. David, bring any kind of card games," Jenie says.

As the night goes on, they feel drowsy and fatigued. Everybody in the room falls asleep when the window is sliding to open without making a noise. Then, three miniature men appear and take Jenie out of the room. They are so agile in their movements that Jenie is outside in a minute and walks to her scooter by herself with her eyes closed like a sleepwalker. Jenie in her sleep drives a scooter to the mountain and she lies down on the wooden bed in the cave.

The morning sunlight comes in through a chink in the cave wall. Jenie wakes up pop-eyed thinking that she should have been with three teens. Soon she hears beautiful voices, "Don't be surprised. We brought you here to say something."

"What? I don't understand. You could talk to me in front of Tony and his friends 'cause they know you. What is it?"

"Well, we're moving soon. Here, we've been very pleased with you since you caught our attention when you were in your early teens. We found you somewhere in town. You were so adorable and nice. We saw you live a tough life without parents, but you seemed to be very positive. So we liked to watch and help you if possible. Now you grew up smart to become a college student on your own. And you get good friends. We're proud of you so much," Ali sings.

"Oh, thank you. Where are you going? I'm so sorry to hear that. Why didn't you come to me earlier than now? Anyway, I'll leave for the college next month, too. Then, are you gonna be nearby?" Jenie asks, smiling.

"We're not sure. But we can watch you from somewhere," Oli sings and grins.

14

Jenie sits alone for a while after miniature man-like figures vanish. She looks around the cave thinking she has to clean up before she leaves for the college. At that moment a message pops up on her cell phone, "Jenie, where are you? You're gone. Text me right now."

"I just had something to do, but I'm finished with it. I'll wait for you and your friends around 10 o'clock at the cafeteria in the mall. I'll buy you brunch in gratitude for what you've done," Jenie texts back.

The mall is crowded with kids who are on a summer break. Before heading to the cafeteria, Jenie checks her wristwatch to see whether she has time to drop by at a store to buy souvenirs for Tony and David and Becky. At a jewelry shop she picks up three gold necklaces for them thinking of them as grateful friends.

Jenie enters the cafeteria waving Tony and his friends. She feels a strong friendship grows among them after the event.

"Guys, I thank you so much for your time and effort. You were really nice, so I brought gifts from my heart. I won't forget your heart as long as I live and I hope to keep in touch with you wherever we live. Here they are!" Jenie holds out her hand.

Tony, David and Becky say at the same time, "Thank you, Jenie. You shouldn't have!"

"We all enjoyed so much and I'm so happy to do things with you. Jenie, we put money we earned yesterday in your checking account. To double check, you'd better check now," Tony says with a big smile.

"Oh, can I have such a big money?" Jenie says with a trembling voice.

And she presses on her cell phone and finds out the money transferred into her checking account.

"Oh, what a lucky girl I am! Thanks again, don't forget I always welcome you with my whole heart," Jenie says with a sweet smile.

They walk around the mall for a while after brunch since Jenie is free on the second day in a row. As the afternoon draws on, David leaves for home with Becky while Jenie gives Tony a ride by scooter. On the way to the cottage, Tony suggests that he'll help clear the wooden bed and a fence off the cave. Jenie drops Tony off at the entrance of the Browns' property.

15

Each day passes fast and the heat in August is lessening little by little. Tony is back into a routine and Jenie seems to be ready to leave for the college. Through texting messages Tony and Jenie tell each other what they're doing. One day when Tony is busy with his online computer course, he gets a message that Jenie comes to the cave to remove the stuff.

On the day Jenie's supposed to come, Tony makes an early start in the morning to the cave with Ben and Ed. He wants to surprise Jenie with his handling of the work. He takes a familiar path and reaches the trail which leads to the cave. Walking along the trail, he remembers a golden necklace Ben found, smiling on his face. "Hey, Ben, do you remember a necklace?"

Tony fiddles with Ben's ear.

Tony walks for a mile or so, but he sees nothing but trees and bushes without any sign of the cave. He continues to walk the trail and stops on the top of the gentle slope, looking at a two lane road ahead of him. At that time he sees Jenie stop her scooter to park. He calls out Jenie waving his hands.

Jenie comes up to Tony in an instant and says, "Oh, Tony, you don't have to come up here. Hello, Ben, Ed." She strokes down Ed's hair.

"Hi, Jenie, it's odd. I couldn't find the cave, so I kept walking and then stopped at the end of trail," Tony says with surprise.

"What do you mean? Let's go... uh, oh, I can't see anything. It should be here. Everything's gone! I can't even see the cave. Oh my gosh! Then the cave wasn't natural? What's happening?" Jenie shouts.

"I get it! Ali and his friends made a cave and... they made the bed, huh? What a dumb girl I am!" Jenie says, looking at Tony in dismay.

Jenie and Tony stand in silence for a while.

Tony breaks the silence and starts to talk. "Speaking of them, they can't be real in our daily life. We haven't seen that kind of living things around the world. I even wonder we all really hung around with them, huh."

"Tony, to tell the truth, I talked with Ali and his friends several days ago in the cave. It was the day I treated brunch to you. They said they were leaving, but I didn't believe it. And they're gone. By the way, I even didn't expect this cleaning. Oh boy, they must be living somewhere we never find," Jenie says plainly.

"Everything that has happened to us feels like a dream. Can we see them again? I already miss them," Tony says giving a hollow smile.

Tony sits on a rock and says, "Um... Jenie, are you ready to go? When are you leaving?"

"Tomorrow. There are things to do in the college town, like getting a part time job, you know," she smiles.

"I see. And I'll miss you a lot in the woods. I know we can see whenever you are free..." Tony says, smiling at Jenie.

When looking at Jenie, Tony put his hand in his pocket grabbing a necklace and takes it out. He opens his palm and says, "Let me ask you about this-- this necklace with a pendant of pellucid oval glass. Did you order this to the clerk to put golden letter 'J' inside the glass?"

"No, I don't know because it was hung on my neck when I was found by a social worker at a facility. Maybe my biological mother left it for me," she says.

"Oh, then you'd better keep it. It may be a sign for her to recognize you " Tony says staring at her.

"Nah... I'm sure that she won't look for me. I've been alone all the time and now you're close to me. I don't have a wish of family reunion anyway," Jenie gives a big smile.

As the noonday sun is on the wane, Tony and Jenie rise to their feet to go their separate ways. They hug each other and Jenie goes to her scooter. Tony sees her off on the spot saying, "Take care, until we meet again. Text me every day."

Jenie waves her hand behind her back holding back her tears. Tony watches her back until Jenie leaves, and turns around to go back home.

"Hey, Ben, Ed, let's go home," Tony says briskly.

On the way home Tony keeps looking at trees and rocks in awe of nature. Thinking of Ali and Eli and Oli, he sees the woods in light of a music box, which is full of stories. Now smelling some odor of freshness on the breeze from the woods, he finds that everything in the woods seems alive with inexplicable spirit.

Tony begins to sing like Ali and his friends, expecting every minute of his stay in the woods with another extraordinary experience in the woods.